The Girl in the Park

The Girl
in the Park

Sabrina R. Wade

authorHOUSE®

AuthorHouse™
1663 Liberty Drive
Bloomington, IN 47403
www.authorhouse.com
Phone: 1-800-839-8640

Published by AuthorHouse   06/07/2012

ISBN: 978-1-4670-0134-2 (sc)
ISBN: 978-1-4670-0135-9 (e)

This book is dedicated to Olga Primary School

Willow Class of 2011

Contents

CONTENTS

Chapter 1

My Home

There was a young girl named Clementina Jones.
She was 9 years old. She had short black Afro- Caribbean
hair in two bunches, soft glossy brown skin, big brown
eyes and a scar on her right cheek. Clementina lived
with her parents Pamela Ona-Banjo and Curtis Jones.
She loved her parents dearly. They meant the whole
world to her.

They lived on a council estate in a one bedroom flat, it was damp and cold and there were cockroaches crawling everywhere. Pamela had three cleaning jobs at different times of the day and Dad was a road sweeper and also had a night job doing security.

Because of this Clementina was responsible for everything that had to be done in the house. She had to cook dinner every night, clean the house, and wash the laundry in the laundrette which was half a mile away from her home. When she got home she had to iron it. She had to do these once a week.

If the jobs weren't done by the time her parents got home, she was punished and was sent to sleep in the bathtub without food to eat.

Clementina went to school every day and sat at the back of the class. She never spoke to anyone, not even her class teacher Ms Mason. When they had group discussions Ms Mason would purposely choose her to answer a question even though her hand wasn't up. But she always understood the work and got her work correct.

Chapter 2

P.E. Lesson

Every week Clemmy didn't bring in her P.E. kit,
Ms Mason would ask and Clementina would just
shake her head. One day Ms Mason got very angry and
shouted at her in front of all of the children in the class.

"I am fed up with you not bringing your P.E. kit . . . if the rest of the class can so can you, it is a part of your learning, you are going to do P.E. in your underwear!" shouted Ms Mason with rage. Clementina started crying and hiding behind the teaching assistant Miss Samuels and pleading,

"Please Miss don't hit me please, please I promise I'll bring it next time!"

"Ok ok Clementina . . . . it's going to be ok, you don't have to do P.E. today," Ms Mason said with a soft calm voice and hugging her. She looked at Miss Samuels with a confused facial expression.

Ms Mason told the children to line up and asked Miss Samuels to bring the children to the sports hall and begin the lesson.

Once Ms Mason calmed Clementina down she asked her some questions.

"I'm sorry I raised my voice Clementina, I never wanted to upset you . . . ." she paused, "what made you think I was going to hit you? I'll never ever do that, it's wrong. No adult is to hit children; if they do they will be in big trouble."

She touched Clementina on her arm and she screamed at the top of her voice. Clemmy showed her arm and there was a huge red burn there. Her arm was red raw and slowly peeling off as she moved the wet flannel away.

"Clementina, how did this happen?" Ms Mason questioned with a shivering voice. She gazed with fear in her eyes and a tear rolling down her cheek.

"My mum poured her coffee on me because I forgot to brush my teeth this morning . . . she was really angry with me," she whispered with worry as she looked down at the floor.

Ms Mason told Clementina to sit down and ran sobbing to the head teacher's office

"Quick Mrs Thompson you need to call an ambulance and call the police, she needs to be taken away from her cruel family. She needs to be loved not tortured." She sobbed and paced up and down in the office fiddling with her fingers.

"What are you talking about?" Mrs Thompson hesitated with worry.
"Animals like them don't deserve children," she criticized.

"Who doesn't deserve children, Ms Mason? STOP just STOP and explain to me what the problem is," said Mrs Thompson.

"They poured boiling hot coffee on her arm and she is in my class in pain."

Mrs Thompson called the ambulance and the police. Clemmy was taken to the hospital with Ms Mason and they were both questioned by the police. When Clementina came out of hospital she was taken to a children's home where she was safe and cared for and treated as a child.

Chapter 3

New Beginning

A couple of months later Clemmy was adopted by a married couple Mrs Mary Davis and Mr Simon Davis who had no children of their own. Clementina went home with her new carers and she was loved and treated as a regular child.

She was so happy to be with them. She had her own bedroom; it had violet and pink wallpaper, a double bed with fluffy cushions and pink netted drapes with silver butterflies. She had the most amazing wardrobe with plenty of new clothes, shoes and dressing up outfits and an endless amount of toys.

She was so excited and overwhelmed with her new life.

Days later the family moved from Essex to London. They moved nearer to Mary's new job. Mary was promoted to a higher position and would be working in the HSBC tower in East London and Dad had also got a new job at Credit Swiss a bank company nearby.

"So Clemmy, do you like your new home? I know that you had just got used to the house in Dagenham. The good thing about this is that we all have a fresh start . . . a new life and a . . . new home." Mum said with an enormous smile on her face, her arms wide open as she embraced Clemmy and Dad with excitement. Clementina looked at both carers and smiled.

"Mummy and Daddy I'm so happy to be with you both," she replied happily.

The morning after

"Sweet heart it's seven o' clock - time to wake up for school." Mum whispered to Clementina as she sat on her bed. Today was her first day at her new school.

"I'm really nervous . . . so if the children don't like me?" she said with worry.

"Don't worry everything is going to be great, just be yourself." said Mum.

So she put on her school uniform, a green and white and navy tartan shirt, navy trousers and black shoes.

Dad dropped her at school. Whilst on their journey she listened to her favourite song on the radio.

13

Sabrina R. Wade

"You're thinkin about being my baby. It don't matter if you're black or white." she sang at the top of voice.

"Right we're here now, everything is going to be great. You will make new friends and meet new teachers. Like mum said to you this morning . . . just be yourself."

Chapter 4

Ring-a-ling

The bell rang and she went into class.

"Come on settle down class, put your book bags in the box and your packed lunches in the other box, then sit down on the carpet please . . . thank you." The class teacher stood at the front of the class by her desk she continued to speak.

"Right class now that we have settled down we have three new children in our class, so make them feel welcome. Firstly we are going to introduce ourselves to the new children . . . right let's sit in a circle," she said with a soft voice.

"Miss it isn't circle time today," a child said in confusion.

"Well Tom today is a very special day," she replied.

"Right I'll go first my name is Mrs James and I'm your class teacher," she said with a calm voice and smiled and her hand placed on her thighs.

Clementina introduced herself then the other two new children.

"Hello, my name is Mohan. I am 9 years old and this is my twin sister," he said with an Indian accent. Keya just smiled at everyone.

"She is shy," he grinned.

So they continued to go round in the circle as the other children introduced themselves. Clementina thought to herself everyone seemed nice and friendly.

"I like this school better than my old school," she whispered to herself with a grin.

"Can I have two volunteers to be buddies?" Miss asked.

The majority of the class put their hand in the air, desperate to be chosen.

"Sammy and Paul, you will be buddies throughout the day. That includes assembly, playtime and showing them to the lavatory. Thank you my super helpers."

"Mrs James seems like a very happy teacher," she thought.

Mrs James had long curly shimmering brunette hair; she was tall and even taller with high heels on and had big brown eyes. Mrs James looked like Vanessa Hudgens from High School Musical. She looked about 35 years old.

Chapter 5

Lunch Time

The day was going really well until lunch time. Sammy and Paul left her and the twins in the lunch hall and went outside with their other mates. Once they had finished they went back to class to sit with Mrs James. She asked them how their day was going and gave them some jobs to do.

"Can you sharpen the colouring pencils please, we are going to do art this afternoon."

"That sounds like fun, what we are going to draw?" Clementina asked.

"Well all of the children in the class would have to draw a picture of something or someone, that means a lot to them and write a sentence why," she explained.

Mohan said that he was going to do a picture of himself and his family and their home where they use to live in India. Keya did a picture of her and her friends in school skipping in the playground.

"Those are my friends Runa, Moyrom, and Anisha." She paused "I really miss back home. I still keep contact with them but it is not the same," Keya said sadly.

"So what are you going to draw Clementina?" Keya asked.

Clementina looked worried for the first time because she had never mentioned her past to anyone not even Mary or Simon. To her the past was the past and it was a past that was best forgotten about. Clementina was quiet for a couple of seconds. Keya asked her again. Clementina panicked and started fiddling with her fingers.

"Are you ok Clementina?" Mrs James asked.

Clementina relaxed herself and smiled.
"I am going to do a picture of me and my family in our new home," she said proudly.

After an exciting afternoon Dad comes to collect her from school.

"So Clemmy, how did it go today?" Dad asked.

whilst driving his prize possession, a black land rover. "It was great, fantastic, no it was better than fantastic it was incredible!" Clementina screeched.

Clementina talked the whole journey home about her day at school and the twins Mohan and Keya.

Clementina had been a pupil at Six Mills Primary School for a term now, and her best friends were Mohan and Keya. They did everything together.They were the best of friends; they didn't play with any of the other children. Some of the children from their class were mean to them because the twins had a different accent, and nobody spoke to Clementina because she was friends with Mohan and Keya. They didn't care because they were the three musketeers and they didn't need anyone else as long as they had each other. But when the school day was over she was all alone. Keya and Mohan lived on the other side of town and had after school activities so they were never invited over because of their busy lives.

Chapter 6

The Park

From her bedroom window, was a beautiful view of the park across the road. She had never been to this park.

"Dad can I go to the park please!" she yelled from her bedroom.

"Do you have any homework to do?" he called from the living room.

"No Dad, I get homework tomorrow . . . so can I go to the park?" she bellowed.

"Of course you can, just make sure you cross at the zebra crossing!" he hollered.

Clementina rushed to get changed into her white shorts and multi-coloured t-shirt. She ran down the stairs and sat on the bottom step to put her pumps on. After that she opened the front door.

"Dad I'm going to the park," she called as she shut the door behind her. She was so excited and she didn't give Dad the time to answer her.

Clementina walked to the zebra crossing and waited for both of the cars on either side and walked across the road. She pushed the big black gates open and was gobsmacked to see how many children were in the park. There were children on the tall wooden climbing frame,four red swings and a pyramid shaped web. There were parents in the park sitting on the park benches laughing and talking to each other.

Clementina walked to the climbing frame slightly nervously because she was about to meet new people.

"What should I say? Who should I go and speak to first? What will they think about me? Where should I go?" she thought to herself.

From afar on the other side of the park, she saw a girl sitting on the grass playing with her doll. So Clementina walked over to the girl, who had straight blond hair and wore a pretty pink dress and was playing happily.

"Hello my name is Clementina, can I play with you?" she asked with her hands behind her back. The young girl stared at Clementina and without saying a word, she got up with her doll and walked away.

After that Clementina saw a group of children playing rounders . . .

Chapter 7

What's your name?

"Can I play?" she asked.

"Yeah you can be on my team . . . . what's your name?" he asked.

"Clementina."

"Cool, my name is Ben. Join the line, we're batting."

And so she joined the line with a smile on her face relieved that she had made new friends. Soon after it was her turn to bat. She hit the ball far out and did a full rounder. All of her team mates cheered her on.

"Go, go, go, go keep going you're nearly there . . . yeeeaaah!" the team surrounded her
screaming and jumping up and down with joy.

They were awesome- the team were unbeatable. This made her very happy; she felt wanted and had friends out of school. She went home and told her parents all about her trip to the park and her new friends.

Next day she went to school and told Mohan and Keya about her new friends. Every day after school she went to the park to play with Ben and her other friends. Being in the park was when she was most happiest. Some days Ben would come over to her house for tea. His mother was friends with Mrs Davis.
One day Clementina went to the park and Ben wasn't there, he went to the park every day. She thought nothing of it and went to play with her other friends Peter and Laura.

"Hiya guys what you playing?" she asked.

"None of your business, we don't want to play with you!" Laura sneered.

"Yeah we don't want to play with you; we're not your friend," Peter added.

Chapter 8

Alone

So Clementina ran to a nearby bench under a tree in a shaded area. She sat on the beach alone bawling and covering her face with her hands.

A young beautiful girl appeared beside her.

"Why are you sad?" questioned a soft voice. The little girl stroked Clementina's hair ever so gently.

Clementina looked up at the girl with tears running down her cheeks. She was very slim with soft brown skin, hazel eyes, black sleek hair, and two plaited pigtails. She wore shiny red ribbons, a checked shirt, trousers and black shoes.

"My two friends Laura and Peter said they're not my friends and they don't want to play with me," she whimpered and snuffled.

"I'll be your friend, we can be bestest friends," replied the girl.

Clementina smiled and agreed.

"Yes, we can be bestest friends for ever and ever." And they hugged.

They continued to sit on the bench and asked each other questions about themselves.

"My name is Emilia and I am 9 years old."

"My name is Clementina and I am 9 years old too."

"I live across the road and I go to Six Mills Primary School." She continues to question Emilia.

"So, what school do you go to and what is your teacher's name?"

"My school is nearby and my teacher's name is Mrs James." answered Emilia.

"No way me too, my teacher's name is Ms James. That is awesome!" she hollered. The two girls talked and talked, question after question. Soon after it was time for Clementina to go home.

"I have to go home now; I'll see you tomorrow . . . are you going home now?"

"My mum is coming to meet me here, but I'll see you tomorrow. Meet me on this bench," she said.

Clementina and Emilia met the same time same place every day except for the weekends, because Emilia had weekend activity clubs.

Chapter 9

Come for Tea

One Wednesday evening after dinner the family sat down in the living room, having a conversation about their day. Clementina spoke about her day in school and what she did in her P.E. lesson. Mum spoke about her day at work.

"It was a nightmare getting to work this morning, there was a train delay on the Docklands Light Railway. I waited for 30 minutes so I decided to walk to work," said Mum

"How long did it take, Mum?" Clementina asked her mother.

"It took me 40 minutes. Thank goodness it was a warm sunny day."

"Well, did you watch the news or listen to the radio?" Dad commented.

"Yes, they announced it on BBC Breakfast News. They said that there was a slight delay . . . how about you?" said mum.

"Well a bit of traffic, just the usual," he said.

"So Clementina how is your friend . . . ."

"Emilia!" she squawked with excitement.

"Yes that's the one, how is Emilia. What did you do in the park today?" he said gracefully.
Before Clementina could answer mum suggested that Emilia should come over for tea.

"Tomorrow when you go to the park, ask Emilia to ask her mother if she would like to come over for tea. It will be nice to finally meet her seeing as you talk about her all the time" mum said.

"Oh mum that is an amazing idea! I can't wait to show her my bedroom and all of my toys. Emilia will like my room because her favourite colour is pink and she likes High School Musical. We can watch my DVD's. What are you going to cook? Can we cook her favourite food?" she said jumping up and down with excitement.

"Slow your horses Clemmy. We haven't got permission from her mother yet," Dad raised his arms above his head and laughed and mum was crying with laughter, with tears streaming on her cheeks.

So the following day after school she went to the park and ran to the bench where Emilia was sitting.

"Emilia my mum asked me to ask you if you'd like to come to my house for tea tomorrow after school," she proposed.

Emilia looked at her with a nervous smile whilst fiddling with her fingers and tapping her left foot on the ground.

"O.k., I'll ask my mum and tell you tomorrow."

"My mum needs the answer today so she can go shopping and get us some treats. When your mum comes to collect you in the park, you and your mum can come to my house so your mum and my mum can be friends, or best friends like me and you," she replied.

"My mum hasn't got the time to meet your mum today because we are busy."

"Why, what are you doing?" Clementina asked with a smirk.

"Well . . . um . . . um . . . we are . . . um . . . going to my Nan's house and . . . um . . . she lives far, far away." She hesitated. Clementina asked Emilia several times to come to her house but always gave the same excuses. This left Clementina sad because she wanted to have a friend to share her toys and watch her DVD's with.

Chapter 10

Mum in the Park

One afternoon Mum walked over to the park to collect Clementina in the park because she did tea slightly earlier than usual. As she walked through the big black gates she saw Clementina sitting on the bench laughing and talking. She was sitting at an angle as if she was facing someone. Mum hid behind the bushes for a couple of minutes, watching her playing. Mum stepped out hoping that Clementina hadn't seen her.

"Hey sweetie it's time to come home now," she said calmly with a smile on her face.

She stood up and introduced her. "Mum, this is my friend Emilia."

Mum stared in despair and confusion because there was nobody there, but she didn't question Clementina about it. She just pretended that she could see her.

"Nice to meet you Emilia, I'm Clemmy's mother. We have to go now. See you another time," Mum whispered and held Clementina's hand as they left the park.

Once they got home and had dinner, mum sent her off to the bathroom to have a wash. Mum sat in the living room and spoke to Dad about what had happened in the park. Dad spoke to Clementina about her day in the park and she said the same as usual. Dad suggested to Mum that they should have a meeting with her class teacher to find out if she talked about Emilia in school.

The next day before school Mum and Dad spoke to Mrs James about how she was getting on in school and who her friends were.

Mum asked if there was a girl named Emilia in her class and Mrs James said no.

That very same day in the afternoon Clementina was helping Mrs James in the class setting up paint pots

43

and art books. Mrs James took the opportunity to ask her about her friend Emilia.

"So Clemmy what do you do after school?"

"I play in the park with my best friend Emilia."

"That's nice. What school does she go to?"

"I don't know which school she goes to, but her uniform is the same colours as mine."

"Does she live near you?"

"Yes she does, but I don't know what street."

"Do you know what her last name is?"

"Wilson . . . Emilia Faye Wilson."

"Oh!" Mrs James gasped and shivered as her body felt cold. She was as white as snow. She was quiet for a couple of minutes as she gazed out of the window not saying a single word. She rubbed both of her hands on her face and sighed.

"I'm just going to the office to make a quick phone call, Clemmy."

"O.k. Mrs James."

Mrs James went to the office and called Mr and Mrs Davis to come for a meeting after school. She then went back to class and continued the day as planned.

Chapter 11

The Meeting

Later that day after school Mr and Mrs Davis came in for the meeting.

"I've called for this meeting to talk about your concerns about Clementina and her friendship with others. Myself and Clemmy had an open conversation about the little girl Emilia. It just so happens the girl that Clemmy plays with in the park is a girl that I used to teach three years ago, and her name was Emilia Faye Wilson. Three years ago Emilia had a tragic accident; she was hit by a car as she crossed the road to go to the park and died on the spot. She was crossing at the zebra crossing and the car in the other lane was going so fast and was too late to stop. A couple of months later her parents moved to Ireland and were never seen again. They had lived opposite the park, They couldn't handle the trauma of living on the same street where their daughter died. There is a memorial plaque on the park bench in her memory. She was such a lovely girl." Her voice began to quiver.

Mr and Mrs Davis were shocked and lost for words. Mr Davis just shook his head and shut his eyes and a tear drop fell on his lap. Mrs Davis sobbed and was wiping the tears away from her cheeks.

Mum suggested that they call Clementina to the meeting and let Mrs James sit her down beside here and talk to her about Emilia. She felt very sad to find out that her best friend was a ghost, but on the other hand she was happy that she had a special friend that was only her friend. As they went home in the car, they all spoke about the meeting and both her parent were reassuring that Clementina was going to be o.k., knowing that her best friend was a ghost. When they got home, they decided to go to the park together to look at the plaque on the bench.

There was silence for a couple of seconds and they all gathered around staring at the bench.

"That is so sad, Emilia was the same age as you Clemmy." Mum paused for a second. "I don't know what I would do without you. Her poor parents," she said as she hugged Clementina.

"Mum . . . Dad can I be alone for a minute with Emilia please," she said sadly.

"Of course sweetie we'll see you at home," Dad replied. So Mum and Dad made their way.

Chapter 12

The Secret is Out

Clementina turned her back to the bench as she waved bye to her parents. As she turned around Emilia was sitting on the bench. So she sat down beside her.

"Hi Emilia, I went to school today and told my teacher all about you. I told her that you are my bestest friend in the world. She told me and my parents that you were a pupil in Six Mills Primary School and she was your teacher three years ago. Me and my parents had a meeting with Mrs James after school this afternoon and she told us about your accident. She said that you were hit by a car as you crossed the road to go to the park and died on the road. And you were crossing at the zebra crossing and the car in the other lane was going so fast and was too late to stop. Is it true?" she said as a tear rolled down her cheek.

"Yes, it's true." She continued "it was a fine sunny afternoon. I was in the kitchen with my Mum and I asked her if I could go to the park. She said yes and my Mum always told me to make sure both cars were stopped before I crossed the road, but that day I was in such a rush to get to the ice cream van first before the other children I just ran across the road," she said with a sad voice.

"So why are you always sitting on the bench?" Clementina asked.

"This was my favourite part of the park. Me and my friend Samantha always played together. We made this area our club house. She was my best friend. We went to the same school and we were in the same class. Mrs James is a great teacher. She made us laugh and she was very good at art," she said with a smile.

"Why are you wearing your school uniform?" Clemmy questioned her.

"Well this what I was wearing when it happened," she replied.

"Where do you live?"

"Well I used to live at 29 Winchester Avenue with my parents and my baby brother Matthew."

"That's my address, that's where I live across the road."
"Wow you lived in my house awesome!" Clemmy interrupted.

"Clementina, it's time for me to leave you now. I must go"

"Go where?" Clemmy replied.
"Now that you know about my past I must leave," she said with a soft voice as her hair swayed in the calm

breeze. As the wind got stronger she began to fade and it got colder and darker and darker.

"I will always remember you Clemmy," she whispered. Sparkly stars circulated around her and then a bright bolt of light shone... the sun shone through the trees on to the plaque on the bench. A reflection of Emilia's face appeared on the golden plaque and she smiled.

"I will miss you." She cried and wiped the tears from her cheeks then made her way home.

Chapter 13

Two Decades Later . . .

Years later Clementina got married and had a daughter of her own. She named her Faye Davis McQueen. They lived at 29 Winchester Avenue with their dog Bo. Faye went to Six Mills Primary School and her class teacher's name was Mrs James. Every day after school Faye would go to the park and play. She had a friend there and her name was Emilia Faye Wilson . . . .